TRINITY
A PLACE FOR THE DAMNED

A **TANTRUM** NOVELLA - COMPANION TO **"NO PLACE FOR THE DAMNED"**

COLIN OCCUPANCE

ACT 1
MANIFEST
DESTINY

CHAPTER 1
A FUTURE UNVEILED

CHAPTER ONE

A FUTURE UNVEILED

June 10, 1945

THE SUN HANGS LOW on the horizon, casting long shadows across the cluttered desk where I now sit, pen in hand. The fading light filters through the grimy window of my cramped, nondescript apartment, catching the motes of dust that dance lazily in the air. It's a modest space, reflecting the transient nature of my existence these past few years—a life uprooted and remade in service to the war effort.

Today, I stand at the threshold of a new beginning, about to embark on a journey that promises to reshape my very existence. A letter arrived this morning, delivered by a sombre-faced courier in the muted khaki of a military uniform. The envelope was unmarked, save for the official government seal that gleamed dully in the wan light. Its contents were cryptic yet tantalising, an invitation to contribute to a project of unparalleled importance—the Manhattan Project. The name alone evokes whispers of mystery and reverence, a promise of secrets waiting to be unlocked.

As I read the letter's enigmatic contents, my mind raced with possibilities. What hidden knowledge awaits me at Los Alamos, that remote outpost of scientific progress? What earth-shattering discoveries might be unearthed in those clandestine laboratories? Excitement courses through my veins as I hastily pack my meagre belongings, the detritus of a life interrupted by the clarion call of duty.

Yet even as I prepare to depart, an undercurrent of unease nips at the edges of my exhilaration. The project's shroud of secrecy, the grave tone of the letter's prose, all hint at a gravity of purpose beyond mere scientific inquiry. I can't shake the feeling that I stand on the precipice of something monumental and terrifying in equal measure. But I know there can be no turning back now. With an unsteady hand, I pen a brief note of acceptance, sealing my fate and that of the world as I know it.

***

The journey to Los Alamos is a blur of rugged, sun-drenched landscapes—a far cry from the urban canyons of my former life. The sprawling complex rises abruptly from the surrounding desert like some alien fortress, all concrete and steel and tightly coiled secrecy. As I step through its heavily guarded gates, I feel the weight of countless eyes upon me—some curious, others wary. The atmosphere crackles with tension and barely suppressed energy, a sense that the very air is charged with the electric potential of the brilliant minds gathered within.

I barely have a chance to settle into my spartan quarters before I'm summoned to my first meeting, a briefing with the enigmatic Dr J Robert Oppenheimer himself. The man is a legend in scientific circles, a towering intellect whose piercing gaze seems to penetrate the very essence of those he encounters. As I take my seat in the dimly lit conference room, surrounded by an eclectic mix of rumpled academics and steely-eyed military men, I feel the full weight of the project's importance settle upon my shoulders.

Oppenheimer speaks in measured tones, his voice soft yet commanding as he outlines the project's staggering scope. The veil of secrecy is slowly lifted, revealing the true nature of the weapon we have been assembled to construct—a bomb of unfathomable destructive power, harnessing the very forces that power the Sun. As he describes the challenges that lie ahead and the magnitude of the undertaking, I feel a mixture of awe and creeping unease. The question rises unbidden in my mind: in our quest to unlock the atom's secrets, what demons might we unleash upon the world?

As I leave the briefing, my mind reeling with the implications of the task before us, I find myself grappling with a fundamental question of morality and responsibility. The Manhattan Project represents the epitome of human ingenuity and scientific progress… but at what cost? As I wander the labyrinthine corridors of the facility, past humming generators and glowing control panels, I can't shake the feeling that we are poised at the edge of a precipice, about to take a leap into an abyss from which there may be no return.

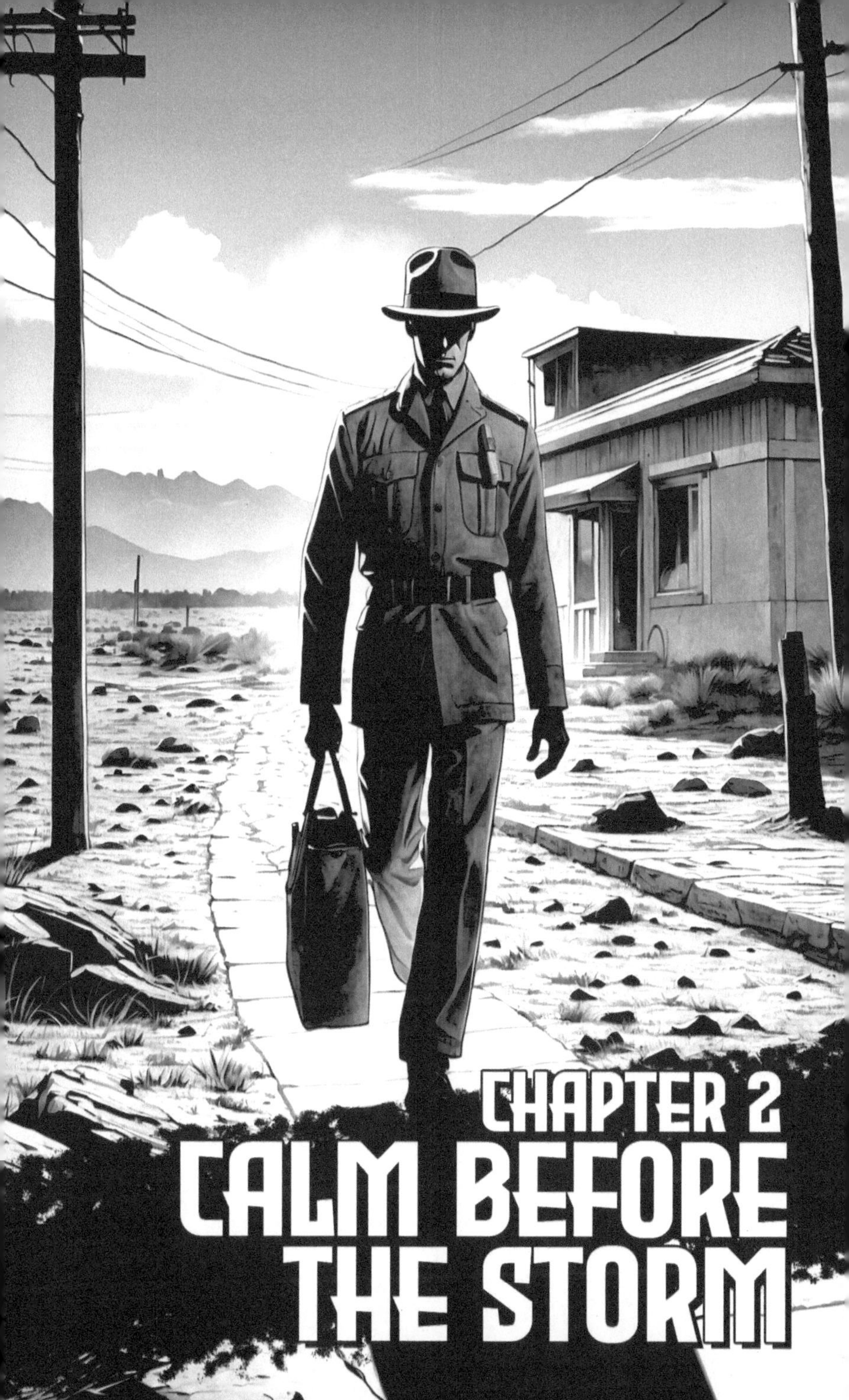
CHAPTER 2
CALM BEFORE
THE STORM

CHAPTER TWO

The Calm Before the Storm

June 23, 1945

I sit hunched over my desk, the single bare lightbulb casting harsh shadows across the scratched and dented metal surface. The detritus of countless late nights is strewn before me—crumpled papers bearing half-formed equations, empty coffee cups ringed with the residue of too many bitter brews, the scattered remains of meals hastily consumed and just as quickly forgotten. The walls of my quarters seem to close in around me, a physical manifestation of the pressure that permeates every waking moment within the confines of Los Alamos.

The past week has been a blur of frenetic activity, a ceaseless cycle of calculations and calibrations, hushed conversations and fevered theorising. The Trinity test looms on the horizon, a date with destiny that seems to approach with the inexorable certainty of a freight train. As the hours tick by, the atmosphere within the compound grows ever more charged, the brilliant minds assembled here working themselves into a state of near-frenzy.

Dr Oppenheimer remains a pillar of calm amidst the rising tide of tension, his hawklike features schooled into an expression of focused determination. In our daily briefings, he exhorts us to maintain our dedication to the cause, even as the weight of our endeavour threatens to crush the breath from our lungs. There is a zealot's fire in his eyes as he speaks of the project's world-altering potential, a sense that he views himself as the high priest of a new scientific order.

The other team members are a study in contrasts, each grappling with the enormity of our task in their own way. Dr Edward Teller, a brilliant physicist with a wild shock of hair and manic energy, seems to thrive on the pressure, his mind spinning out ever more audacious theories and hypotheses. Dr Hans Bethe, a quiet and introspective man with a gentle disposition, carries himself with an almost mournful dignity as if he alone comprehends the true cost of our pursuit. And then there is Dr Klaus Fuchs, the enigmatic German émigré with piercing blue eyes and a reserved demeanour that belies a simmering intensity, setting my nerves on edge.

In the project's early days, I easily convinced myself that our work was a necessary evil, a terrible weapon forged in the name of a greater good. But as the reality of the bomb takes shape before our eyes, I cannot help but wonder if we have strayed from the path of righteousness. What price victory if it comes at the cost of our very humanity?

Outside my window, the desert stretches to the horizon, an ocean of shifting dunes and twisted scrub under a merciless sun. The molten desert sands shimmer in the heat, a reminder of the unforgiving nature of this place. There is a strange, alien beauty to the landscape, a sense of nature's raw power barely held in check. But even the desert's vast expanse seems to pale in comparison to the forces we are unleashing within the walls of Los Alamos. As I gaze out over this harsh terrain, I cannot shake the feeling that we are tinkering with primal forces beyond our comprehension—forces that, once unleashed, may consume us all in their unquenchable hunger.

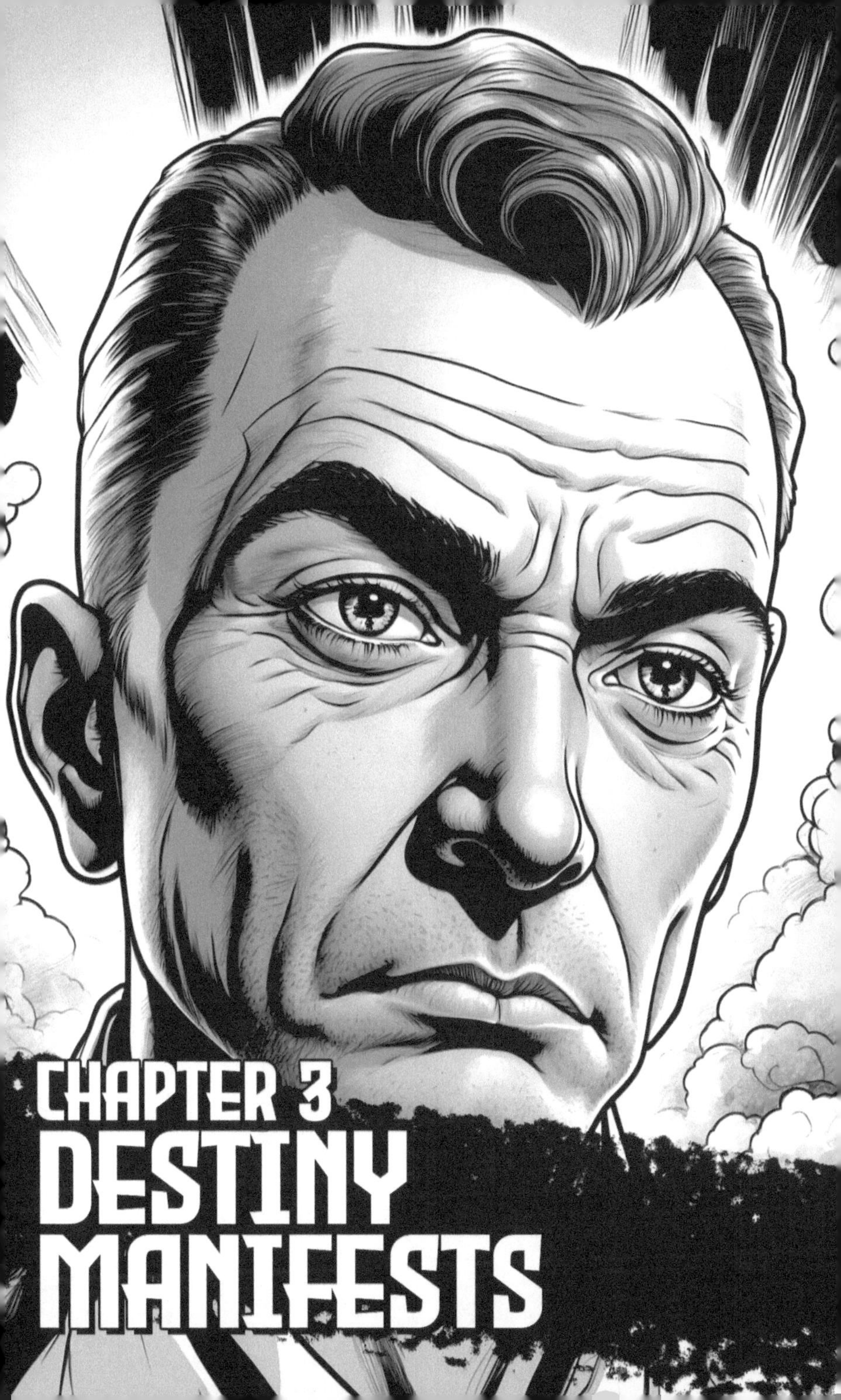
CHAPTER 3
DESTINY
MANIFESTS

CHAPTER THREE

Destiny Manifests

July 16, 1945

The day has dawned with a sense of portentous significance, the first rays of the Sun setting the desert ablaze in a wash of blood-red light. The normally bustling confines of Los Alamos are eerily subdued, the halls echoing with the soft tread of feet and the murmur of hushed conversations. The atmosphere hangs thick with a sense of anticipation mingled with dread, as if the air is charged with the momentous import of what is to come.

I find myself strangely calm amidst the rising tide of tension, my mind clear and focused despite the maelstrom of conflicting emotions that churn within me. In these final hours before Trinity, I feel the weight of history pressing down upon us all, the sense that we stand on the threshold of a new era—one that will be defined by the awesome power we are about to unleash.

***

As I make my way through the winding corridors of the facility, I cannot help but marvel at the sheer scope of the project we have undertaken. Every room and hallway is a hive of activity, scientists and engineers working with feverish intensity to ensure that every last calculation is checked and every contingency accounted for. The scale of the operation is staggering, a testament to the incredible complexity of the task at hand.

I pause outside the door to Dr Oppenheimer's office, steeling myself for what I know will be a momentous conversation. The man who has become the face of the Manhattan Project is a study in contrasts—brilliant and driven, yet haunted by the weight of the responsibility he bears. As I enter the room, I find him hunched over his desk, his face cast in shadow and lined with worry.

"It's almost time," he says softly, his eyes fixed on some distant point beyond the confines of the room. "All our work, all our sacrifices… it all comes down to this moment."

I nod slowly, the gravity of his words settling over me like a leaden cloak. "Do you think we're ready?" I ask, my voice sounding small and insignificant in the face of the monumental task ahead.

Oppenheimer looks up at me, his gaze intense and searching. "We have to be," he replies, his voice ringing with a steely determination. "The fate of the world hangs in the balance. We cannot afford to fail."

I feel a chill race down my spine at the utter certainty in his words, the sense that he sees himself as an instrument of destiny, a man chosen by fate to reshape the course of human history. And yet, beneath the unwavering resolve, I detect a flicker of something else—a hint of doubt, perhaps, or the faintest glimmer of regret for the terrible knowledge we have unleashed upon the world.

As I take my leave of Oppenheimer's office, I cannot shake the feeling that I have just witnessed a man struggling under the weight of an almost unbearable burden. The responsibility we bear is a heavy one, a yoke that threatens to crush the life from us all. And yet, there can be no turning back now. The wheels of fate are in motion, and we are all inexorably carried along in their wake.

***

The hours crawl by with agonising slowness; each second stretched taut with the weight of anticipation. And then, at last, the moment arrives. The convoy of Willys MBs and transport trucks rumbles out of Los Alamos, snaking its way through the desert wilderness to the test site at Alamogordo. The air is thick with a sense of tense expectation, the assembled scientists and military personnel moving with a grim sense of purpose.

As we arrive at Trinity, I am struck by the sheer scale of the apparatus before us—the towering steel scaffolding, the massive sphere of the bomb itself, suspended like some malevolent eye at the centre of a web of cables and wires. The early morning light casts long shadows across the desert floor, the chill of the pre-dawn air raising goosebumps on my skin.

***

The final countdown begins, the voice of Dr Oppenheimer echoing over the loudspeakers with a grave solemnity. In those last breathless seconds, I feel my heart pounding in my chest, my mouth dry from fear and exhilaration. And then, with a blinding flash and a roar that seems to shake the very foundations of the earth, the world changes forever.

The brilliant light of the explosion sears itself into my retinas, a sight that will be forever etched into my memory. As the mushroom cloud blooms over the desert like some monstrous flower, I feel a sense of awe mingled with horror. In this moment, I know with terrible certainty that the dawn of a new age has surely begun, that we have unleashed a power beyond our ability to control—a force that will shape the destiny of nations for generations to come.

In the stunned silence that follows, I hear Dr Oppenheimer's voice, soft and haunted, reciting a line from the ancient Hindu scripture: "Now I am become Death, the destroyer of worlds." The words hang in the air like a portent, a grim prophecy of the dark future that we have wrought. As I stand there amidst the devastation, surrounded by the fruits of our terrible labour, I cannot help but wonder if we shall ever truly comprehend the magnitude of what we have done.

CHAPTER 4
THE WEIGHT OF
CONSEQUENCE

CHAPTER FOUR

The Weight of Consequence

July 25, 1945

In the days since Trinity, a pall of unease has settled over Los Alamos, a miasma of doubt and recrimination that seeps into every corner of the facility. A grim, funereal silence now haunts the once-bustling halls, the faces of the scientists and engineers etched with the same shell-shocked expression I see staring back at me from the mirror each morning.

I try in vain to lose myself in the cold comfort of numbers and equations. The single, grimy window above my bunk filters the harsh glare of the desert sun, casting the room in a pallid, sickly light—a fitting ambience for the gnawing guilt and uncertainty that eats away at my troubled mind.

Dr Oppenheimer moves among us like a ghost, his once-proud bearing stooped under the weight of terrible knowledge. In furtive whispers, the other scientists speak of secret meetings and heated arguments behind closed doors, a fierce battle for the soul of the project. Oppenheimer pleads for restraint, a voice of conscience railing against the juggernaut of military expedience. Yet it is a losing battle, I fear. The gravity of consequence has been unleashed in all its fearsome necessity.

Even as the spectre of Hiroshima looms on the horizon, a portent of the terrible devastation we are poised to inflict, I find myself questioning the very foundations of our venture. In the heady early days of the project, it was easy to lose oneself in the thrill of discovery, to wrap ourselves in the illusion that we were soldiers of science, marching toward a brighter future. But now, with the terrible reality of our creation made manifest, the scales have fallen from my eyes. Have we, in our relentless pursuit of progress, unwittingly embarked upon a Faustian plan, trading our moral compass for the seductive promise of power and knowledge? Are the echoes of our innocence being silenced by our own pride and ambition?

I find my gaze drawn often to the barren expanse of the desert beyond the compound walls, the harsh beauty of that timeless landscape offering a strange solace. In the face of the enormity of our actions, the vast indifference of nature seems almost comforting. The world will endure, even if we damn ourselves in the name of scientific progress.

Internally, I cannot escape the weight of the choices we have made. In unleashing the power of the atom, we have set in motion a chain reaction that will shape the course of human destiny, for good or for ill. The die has been cast, the path chosen, and it falls to us now to navigate the perilous road ahead.

But even as I grapple with the moral implications of our work, I cannot help but feel a sense of awe at the sheer audacity of our work. In a sense, we are wrestling death from the divine, seizing control of the fundamental forces of creation and destruction that have always been the sole purview of the gods. It is an intoxicating and terrifying prospect, one that fills me with both exhilaration and dread.

As I lay down my pen, exhausted by the turmoil of my thoughts, I am filled with a grim resolve. Come what may, I will see this terrible and wondrous project through to its conclusion. The weight of consequence is ours to bear, the burden of our dreadful knowledge ours to carry. And in this shattered, hopeful world we have wrought, we must find the strength to endure.

In the end, I am left to ponder the legacy we are leaving for future generations. Will they consider this moment a turning point in human history, the dawn of a new age of discovery and progress? Or will they curse our names, condemning us for unleashing the forces of destruction upon an unsuspecting world? Only time will tell. But one thing is certain: we have opened Pandora's box, and there can be no turning back now. We can only hope that, in the end, the light of knowledge and understanding will triumph over the darkness of fear and destruction. For in this brave new world we have created, it is the only hope we have left.

ACT 2
A HELLBOUND PLANET

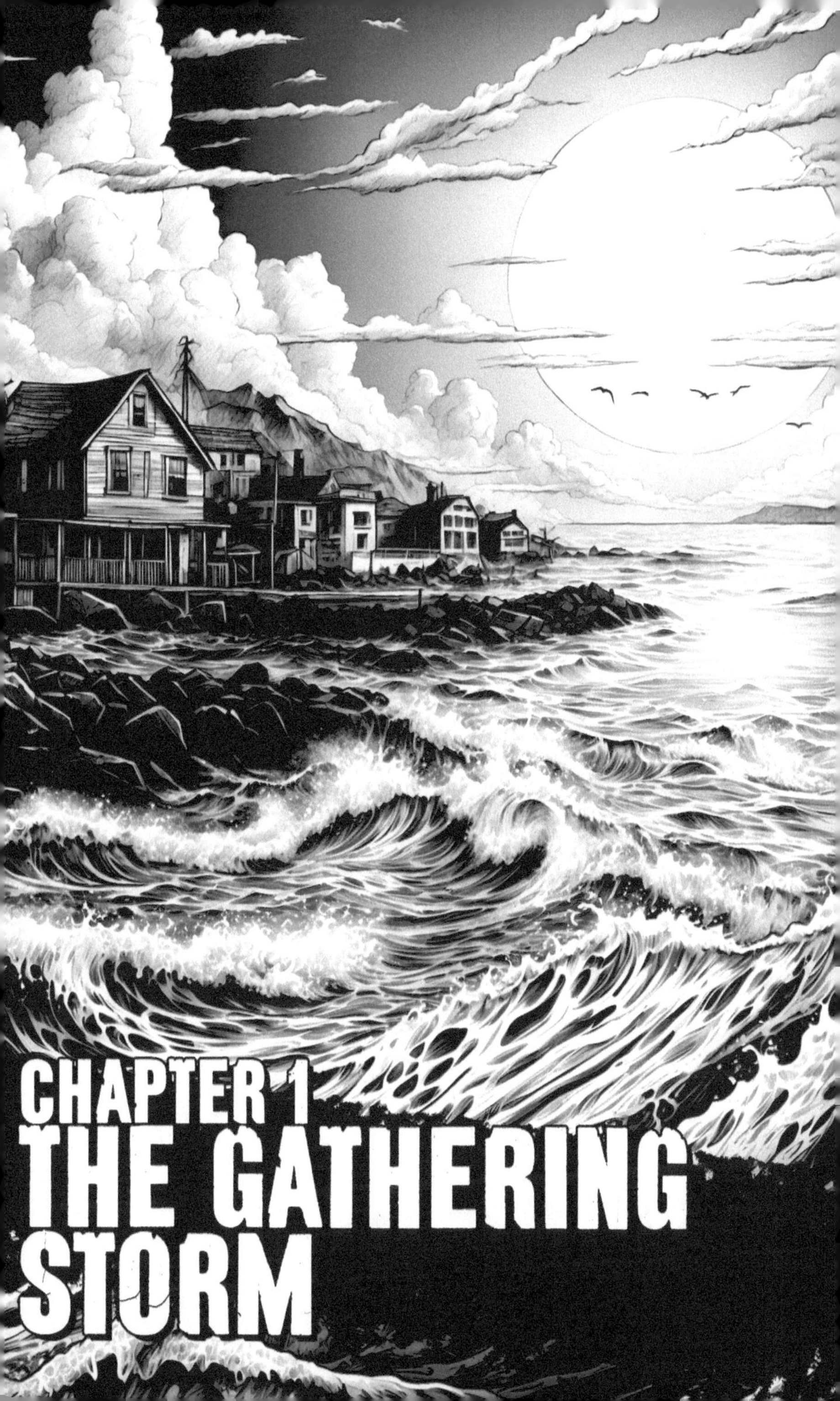
CHAPTER 1
THE GATHERING
STORM

ONE

THE GATHERING STORM

IT STARTED WITH SUBTLE signs at first. Winters that seemed a little warmer, summers a touch more sweltering. Glaciers receding a bit faster, sea levels rising an inch higher. Most people were too busy going about their daily lives to really notice or care. But the scientists saw what was happening. They had been ringing the alarm bells for years about climate change, about the dangerous path humanity was on. But oil companies with billions in profits, industries with products to sell, and politicians with campaigns to fund muddied the waters, sowing doubt and confusion to delay action.

"It's just part of the Earth's natural cycles," they claimed. "The science is unsettled. We need more research before upending our economy over this."

But the science was clear. Atmospheric CO2 levels were the highest they'd been in millions of years. Global temperatures were already up by more than 1°C since pre-industrial times, with more warming locked in. The oceans were acidifying as they absorbed excess carbon. Ice sheets the

size of countries were melting into the sea. Extreme floods, fires, and storms were becoming more frequent. The signs were everywhere if you cared to look. Or dared.

Some governments began taking modest steps—

investments in renewable energy, efficiency standards, and emissions reduction targets. But it was too little, too late. The world was still addicted to fossil fuels. Coal, oil, and natural gas still provided the vast majority of humanity's energy. Sprawling cities, gas-guzzling cars, disposable lifestyles—society was built around the assumption of endlessly burning carbon. Changing course felt unimaginable.

So, we continued sleepwalking toward disaster. The warnings from scientists grew louder and more dire. Environmentalists protested and pleaded for action. Children held strikes, imploring leaders to safeguard their future. But the gears of the global economy churned on, demanding sacrifice at the altar of growth. Fossil fuel companies planned new oil fields, pipelines and coal plants. The carbon already in the atmosphere trapped more heat. Permafrost thawed, releasing methane. Wildfires turned forests from carbon sinks to carbon sources. Feedback loops began amplifying and accelerating warming.

A terrifying realisation began to dawn: we were running out of time. The window to avert catastrophe was slamming shut. Business as usual was a death sentence for civilisation, if not humanity itself. Incremental change within a fundamentally unsustainable system wasn't enough. We needed a WWII-scale mobilisation, a complete redesign of society practically overnight. But how? The political will wasn't there. Powerful forces, guided by greed's desire, were arrayed against it. We were locked into a status quo that was devouring our future. Something had to give.

The signs of the impending catastrophe were everywhere, but most people chose to look the other way. Those who sounded the alarm were drowned out by a chorus of denial and misinformation. Politicians beholden to fossil fuel interests insisted that the economy mattered more than the environment. Pundits on TV mocked the "alarmists" and claimed that a little warming would actually be good for us. Oil and coal companies poured millions into PR campaigns to sow doubt about the science, even as their own research confirmed the truth.

But the physics didn't care about spin or lobbying or quarterly profits. The greenhouse gases kept accumulating in the atmosphere, trapping ever more heat. The ice kept melting, the sea levels kept rising, and the forests kept burning. It was like watching a slow-motion train wreck, knowing exactly where the track led but powerless to stop it.

Some held out hope for a technological silver bullet. Carbon capture to suck the excess CO2 out of the air. Solar radiation management to artificially cool the planet. Fusion power to provide limitless clean energy. But these were all pipe dreams, perpetually a decade or two away from viability. The only real solution was the one that was politically and economically impossible: to radically change our way of life. To end the age of fossil fuels and consumerism and growth at all costs.

A few countries tried to lead the way. A carbon tax here, a green 'new deal' there. But it was too little, too late. The global economy was still hopelessly dependent on cheap oil and coal. Developing nations pointed out the hypocrisy of the West denying them the same dirty industrialisation that had made it rich. Geopolitical tensions flared as nations jockeyed for control of dwindling resources. The international cooperation necessary to tackle a threat like climate change remained hopelessly out of reach.

As the impacts worsened, so did the excuses. "It's China's

fault, look how much they pollute!" "The Earth has been through changes before; we'll adapt!" "God won't let his creation be destroyed!" The mental contortions grew ever more absurd. For many, outright denial gave way to fatalistic acceptance. So what if Miami was underwater and the Sahara reached Europe? Pour another drink, crank the AC, and enjoy the end of days.

However, retreating into hedonism or nihilism was a luxury not everyone could afford. In the Global South, millions were already being displaced by drought, famine, and rising tides. Climate refugees streamed across borders, straining societies to the breaking point. Failed states and civil wars multiplied. The imbalance between the haves and have-nots grew into a yawning chasm, sowing the seeds of chaos and unrest.

Those who could read the writing on the wall started making preparations. The rich bought up land in places like New Zealand and Patagonia, building bunkers and stockpiling supplies. Governments quietly drew up plans for martial law and population control. The most forward-thinking elites began looking beyond Earth itself, convinced that escape was the only way to avoid the coming cataclysm.

And so, as the world careened blindly toward the abyss, a select few were already laying the groundwork for a new future. One where humanity would not be bound to a single fragile planet, forever at the mercy of its own worst impulses. One where the hard lessons of Earth's demise could be etched into the very foundations of society, never to be forgotten.

But first, the collapse had to run its course. The old order had to crumble before something new could rise in its place. The age of fire, flood, and famine was only just beginning. The real trials still lay ahead.

CHAPTER 2
INEVITABILITY

TWO

INEVITABILITY

Dr Vihaan Gupta, a brilliant astrophysicist with a keen intellect and a troubled conscience, rubbed his temples, bloodshot eyes staring at the graph on his screen. Though only in his late thirties, the weight of the world's fate had etched premature lines into his handsome brown face. The lines of atmospheric CO2 and average global temperature continued their frightening upward climb, like a roller coaster with no brakes barreling toward a cliff. He'd seen these numbers countless times before and run the models repeatedly. But it never got easier to face the horrifying truth they foretold.

His lab partner, Dr Erik Johansen, a tall, lean Scandinavian with an athletic build and a perpetually worried expression, burst into their cramped university office, face flushed. "Have you seen this?" He thrust a new study in front of him. "Greenland and Antarctica are melting faster than we thought. Several meters of sea level rise could be locked in already."

Vihaan sighed heavily. "Just add it to the list. We blew past 450ppm CO2 last month. This summer's heat waves killed tens of thousands. Crop yields are down twenty per cent in some regions. Insect populations have collapsed. The Amazon is nearing a tipping point where it turns into savanna. I don't know how much more of this I can take."

Erik slumped into a chair, head in his hands. "You'd think the string of Cat 6 hurricanes last year would've been a wakeup call. Or the millions of climate refugees. But emissions are still rising. Nobody is treating this like the existential emergency it is."

"Because the fossil fuel industry has half the politicians in their pockets," Vihaan spat bitterly. "They've known the science for decades. But they valued their profits over the fucking planet. They should be tried for crimes against humanity."

"I'm starting to think we need to consider… other options," Erik said quietly. "The kind of drastic action required may not be possible within our current systems. Governments controlled by corporations interested in keeping their assets valuable, mass media beholden to advertising revenue, a society hooked on endless consumption… Conventional approaches are failing."

Vihaan raised an eyebrow. "What are you suggesting? Sabotage? Eco-terrorism?"

"I don't know," Erik admitted. "Something to break the gridlock. To sound the alarm at a volume they can't ignore. Because we're losing the war here, badly. We don't have unlimited chances to get this right."

Vihaan stared out the window at the orange-tinged sky, the air thick with smoke from distant wildfires. He recalled a line from James Hansen's decades-old paper:

"Imagine a giant asteroid on a direct collision course with Earth. That is the equivalent of what we face now, yet we dither."

But there was no Hollywood action hero to swoop in and nuke the asteroid this time—just the slow, inexorable grinding of physics, chemistry, and biology. The Earth would survive, in some form, as it had for billions of years. The question was whether human civilisation would. And right now, the odds weren't looking good.

Dr Gupta felt an unusual sense of clarity as he studied the grim graphs and models on his screen. The path forward was obvious now, even if it was one he had long resisted. There could be no more half-measures or wishful thinking. The only hope for his species lay in the uncharted void of space.

He reached out to a small network of like-minded colleagues, those who had also begun to lose faith in the possibility of reform on Earth. In private, encrypted channels, they began to flesh out an audacious plan. To create a new branch of human civilisation, one with the wisdom and foresight to learn from the tragedy of its origins.

It was a gamble fraught with astounding hubris. But what waits in the dark is one last chance, however slim, to get it right. Our science showed the signs—we'd all be left behind to pay the price if they failed. If they were to have any legacy at all beyond a toxic planet orbiting a dying star, this might be it—the flickering spark of a species determined not to go quietly into the night.

CHAPTER 3
NOVATERRA

THREE

NOVATERRA

Dr Vihaan Gupta strode into the emergency conference, stacks of papers clutched in his arms. The dozen other scientists from around the world were already seated around the long wooden table, murmuring amongst themselves. He dropped the pile in front of him with a resounding thud.

Let's not mince words," he began without preamble. "We're fucked."

Silence fell across the room. Dr Erik Johansen, seated beside him, nodded grimly.

"The situation is far worse than what is being presented publicly," Vihaan continued. "We've underestimated the rate of change at every turn. Planetary boundaries are being breached left and right. The predictions made decades ago are coming true, but faster than expected and all at once."

He clicked to the first slide, showing a map of global temperatures. Angry splotches of dark red covered most of the Earth's surface.

"We've already locked in over 2°C of warming, likely more," he explained. "That means the coral reefs are doomed. Most of the world's coastal cities will have to be abandoned. Extreme heat will render large swaths of the planet uninhabitable. Breadbaskets will turn to dust bowls. Wars will break out over dwindling resources. Billions will suffer."

He flipped to the next slide, a line graph of various tipping points. "But it gets worse. We're seeing signs that the Amazon rainforest is starting to collapse, decades ahead of schedule. At this rate, it will be gone in fifteen to twenty years. Gone. That alone could add another 1.5°C of warming. The permafrost across Canada and Siberia is rapidly thawing, releasing vast stores of methane. The oceans are losing their ability to act as a carbon sink. Ice sheets are in full-scale meltdown. These feedbacks threaten to rapidly accelerate warming to levels incompatible with organised human civilisation."

Vihaan could see the colour drain from the other scientists' faces as the information sunk in. He paused, letting the awful gravity hang in the air.

"So that's the bad news," he said finally. "The question is, what do we do about it? I've asked you all here today because you're the top minds in your fields. If anyone can figure out how we avoid the total collapse of society and possible extinction of our species, it's us."

An uneasy murmur rippled through the room. Dr Lena Ivanov, a severe-looking Russian woman with steely grey eyes and a no-nonsense demeanour, spoke up first, her voice laced with a heavy accent.

"We're well past the point of half measures," she declared. "The world needs to end fossil fuel use immediately and by any means necessary. Overthrow governments, dismantle corporations, nationalise energy—we no longer have the luxury of gradualism."

Dr Hiroto Nakamura, a soft-spoken Japanese man with a kind face and a brilliant mind for engineering, raised his hand politely, his expression pensive. "With respect, we must focus on mitigation and adaptation to the warming already locked in. Hardening cities against floods, developing resilient crops, geoengineering to reduce solar radiation. Emissions cuts alone won't stave off disaster."

"We're being reactive!" interjected Erik. "Only dealing with consequences, not causes. The scale of the crisis demands an entirely new paradigm. One *not* based on exploitation, extraction, growth. A total reorganisation of society and the economy. Perhaps starting over."

Vihaan held up a hand, quieting the chatter. "These are all… fascinating ideas. But I fear we are thinking too small. Even your most radical proposals are band-aids for a sucking chest wound. We're still talking about working within systems that are fundamentally broken. Reforming institutions resolutely incapable of change at the scale and speed required."

He leaned forward, face deadly serious. "I believe we need to start considering the unthinkable. The possibility that there is no way to salvage our current civilisation. That continuing on this planet has become a dead end for humanity. That our only hope… may lie in the stars."

A ripple of reactions swept through the room. Some shifted uncomfortably in their seats, brows furrowed in scepticism. Others exchanged glances with their neighbours, whispering under their breath. A few even let out muffled, incredulous laughs. But despite the mixed response, a heavy silence soon settled over the group as the weight of Vihaan's words sank in.

Dr Arjun Rao, a distinguished Indian gentleman with a neatly trimmed beard and a regal bearing, finally broke the silence, his rich baritone voice filling the room. "Vihaan, what are you suggesting?"

He took a deep breath. "I'm suggesting we need an escape plan—a way to preserve human civilisation's most essential knowledge and capabilities somewhere off Earth. A 'backup' of our species, if you will, in case the worst comes to pass. It may sound like science fiction, but I assure you, the situation is dire enough to warrant considering such extreme measures."

He clicked to the next slide, showing an image taken by the James Webb Space Telescope of Enceladus, the ice-covered moon of Saturn. The conference room erupted.

The room buzzed with a mix of excitement and disbelief as Dr Vihaan Gupta laid out his audacious proposal. He clicked through a series of slides, each revealing more details about the clandestine project he called "NovaTerra."

"We've been working on this for years, in partnership with space agencies and private industry around the world," he explained. "The technology for long-distance space travel and terraforming has advanced rapidly in recent decades, thanks to propulsion, life support systems, and bioengineering breakthroughs. We are confident that we now have the capability to send humans to Saturn's moons and transform barren worlds into habitable ones."

He showed designs for sleek, self-contained pods that could sustain a person in cryosleep for years, decades, or even centuries. Genetically engineered crops and microbes that could thrive in alien soils. Robotic drones that could construct habitats and infrastructure autonomously. It was like something from a science fiction novel, but Vihaan insisted it was all based on cutting-edge research and prototypes.

"The plan is to send a first wave of pods to Enceladus, the most promising candidate for near-term habitability," he continued. "It's believed that a vast liquid ocean exists beneath its icy surface, kept warm by tidal forces and potentially harbouring the ingredients for life. Once there, the pioneers will begin the process of drilling through the ice, seeding the ocean with tailored lifeforms, and building a sustainable colony. More waves will follow as the settlement grows and stabilises."

Lena's eyes widened as she processed the magnitude of Vihaan's words. She leaned back in her chair, a mixture of disbelief and resignation flickering across her face. "This all sounds very impressive, but how do you propose to fund and execute such a massive undertaking without the public knowing? The scale is far beyond any space mission in history."

Vihaan hesitated, then sighed. "You're right, Lena. The truth is, this project is already well underway. It has been for years, hidden behind shell companies and black budgets. Trillions have been secretly diverted from military expenditures and stimulus packages—the cogs have been turning since we first heard the bell toll for mass extinction. NovaTerra is the real reason billionaires have been pouring money into private space ventures. It's an open secret among the power brokers that our world is doomed. If word of this ever got out to the general public, there would be chaos and uprising. But those in power have decided that the risk is worth it for the sake of preserving some remnant of humanity."

Frenzied crosstalk filled the room as the assembled experts grappled with the implications. Vihaan held up a hand for silence.

"I know this is a lot to take in," he said solemnly. "And I won't pretend there aren't thorny ethical questions involved. But the cold equations are clear—humanity as we know it cannot survive the coming collapse. Enceladus is our best hope for a lifeboat, a place where we can preserve and rebuild. The alternative… is extinction."

The room fell into a sobered hush. Finally, Dr Erik Johansen broke the silence.

"I dedicated my life to trying to save this planet," he said hoarsely, his voice cracking. "Every waking moment, for decades. But I see now that I was fighting a losing battle. Perhaps, in the long arc of time, our purpose was always to be the bridge between worlds, to carry the light of consciousness beyond the Earth. If this is to be our final act… then let us make it one worthy of remembrance."

Vihaan nodded grimly. "Well said, Erik. We have a long road ahead of us, and many challenges to overcome. But today, let us commit ourselves fully to the task at hand. To the brave new world waiting to be born out there in the dark. To NovaTerra—our last, best hope."

As the scientists filed out of the conference room, abuzz with purpose and trepidation, Vihaan couldn't help but feel a twinge of regret. Regret for the world they were abandoning to its fate, for the loved ones who would be left behind. But he steeled himself with the knowledge that this was the only way. The only path that offered some glimmer of a future for his species.

And so, with heavy hearts and determined minds, they set to work on the most audacious project in human history. The race was on to build an interstellar lifeboat before the clock ran out. The fate of humanity now rested in their hands.

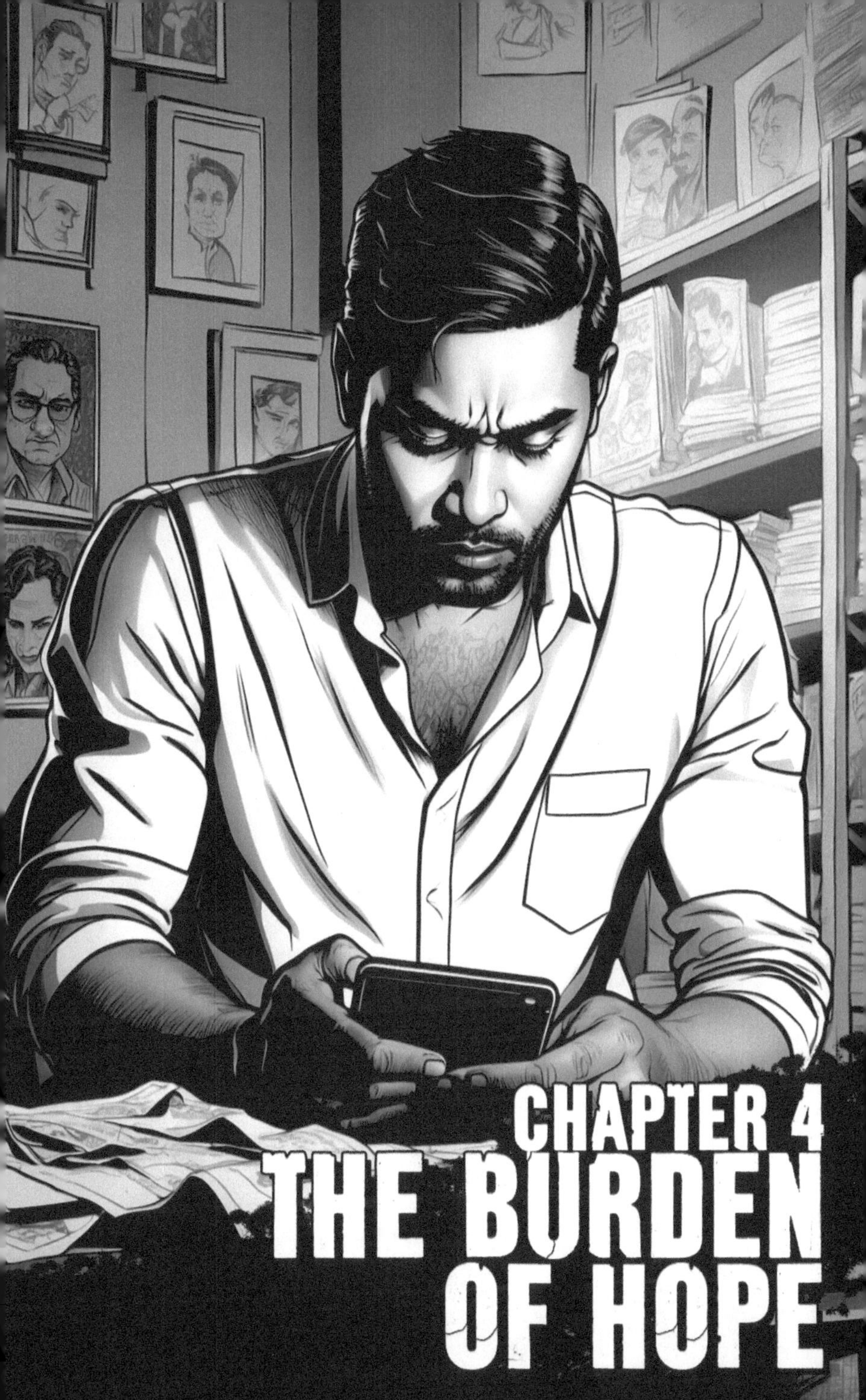

CHAPTER 4
THE BURDEN OF HOPE

FOUR

THE BURDEN OF HOPE

October 7, 2043

Dr Vihaan Gupta's Diary Entry

The NovaTerra Project. A last-ditch effort to save something of ourselves before it was too late. Twenty thousand pods, each carrying a single traveller and the cumulative knowledge of human civilisation, launched on a one-way journey to seed a new world. Enceladus, the frozen moon of Saturn, covered in a crust of ice hiding a dark liquid ocean. It was the only way. Earth had finally reached the point of no return.

I still remember that emergency convention like it was yesterday. I had long argued such drastic measures might become necessary, but to hear government ministers, captains of industry, and military brass discuss the end of the world so matter-of-factly... it chilled me to the bone. They pored over the dismal projections, the point of no return. How long could modern society expect to last as critical planetary boundaries were breached? It was clear our cosmic lifeboat would have to launch within five years at most to have any chance of success.

Enceladus was chosen over Proxima Centauri b. Both were potentially habitable, but Enceladus could be reached in six to eight years with existing propulsion technology. Proxima Centauri b was likely more suited to humanity's needs but would take millennia. We'd need every last second to establish a foothold before the lights went out on Earth.

"Obviously, the public cannot be made aware," the stern-faced three-star general declared. "It would cause widespread panic, a complete breakdown of civil order. We'll divert black budget funding to fast-track construction."

The Pope argued to include all of humanity in a lottery to select the lucky few: democracy and egalitarianism were promptly dismissed as naïve. This mission was too important to leave to chance. Only the best and brightest would be selected. A new technocratic society, built upon rationality and empirical truth, not the madness and folly that brought ruin to Earth. I was chosen as one of them.

In the end, no one could agree on who to blame. The oil barons and their obstructionist lackeys? The feckless politicians kicking the can down the road? A public all too happy to keep consuming? It was so much easier to look to the stars, to pin our hopes on a fresh start light years away.

As the pods were prepped and final systems checks run, I took one last walk through the facility gardens. The vibrant flowers and greenery stood in stark contrast with the climate-ravaged world outside, scorched and lifeless. It occurred to me that this might be the last glimpse of Earthly nature I'd ever see. What a tragic failure of our species, that we rendered our only home hostile to life and had to flee to the void. A world we'd only borrowed, destroyed through consumption.

The worst part is not being able to say goodbye. To leave no message for my wife, to thank my mother for supporting me in my chosen field when my father insisted I follow the family tradition and become a surgeon, to tell my brother his rants about a shadowy continuity of government plan were right all along. To confess that their unchosen loved ones will inherit a dying world, abandoned, while we abscond to the stars. There will be no closure, no reckoning. Just the desperate hope that next time, light years away, we'll learn from our mistakes before it's too late.

ACT 3
THE TRAVELLERS

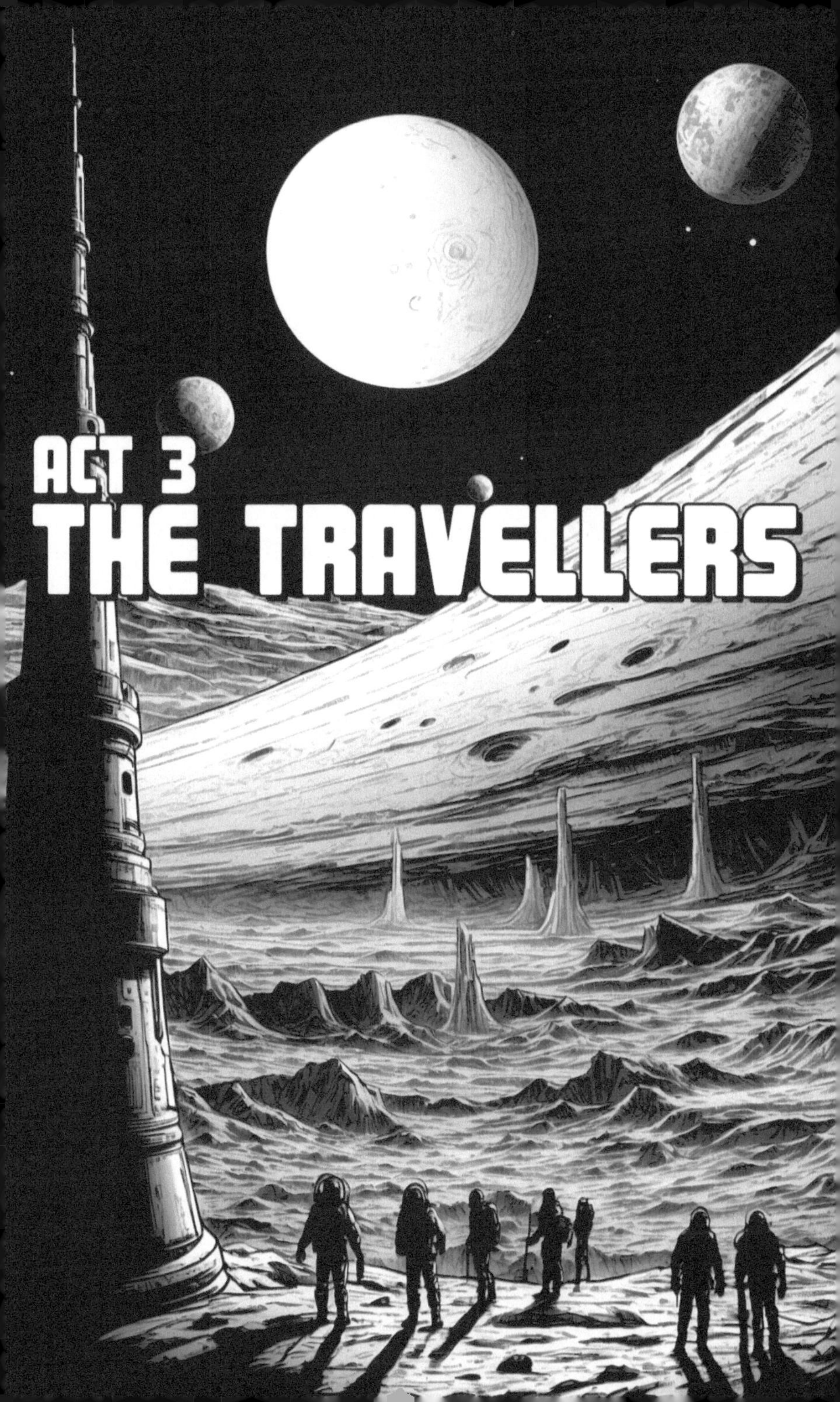

CHAPTER 1
THE LABYRINTH

ONE

THE LABYRINTH

In the heart of the NovaTerra Project, deep within the central command hub, a flurry of activity consumed the control room. Technicians and scientists alike scurried about, making final preparations for the impending launch, now just three months away. Across the globe, hidden beneath the surface, a network of launch facilities lay in wait, each one a sprawling labyrinth of corridors, barracks, and training zones designed to prepare the "Terranauts" for their monumental journey.

These chosen few, numbering twenty thousand strong, had been selected from the world's best and brightest. Some were brilliant scientists and engineers, their minds holding the key to humanity's future. Others were athletes of the highest calibre, their physical prowess ensuring the strength and endurance of the new colony. Still others were artists, musicians, and historians, tasked with preserving and perpetuating the rich tapestry of human culture.

For months, they had trained tirelessly, learning the intricacies of cryosleep and the challenges that awaited them on Enceladus. They were told of the automated systems that would guide their pods, of the advanced technology that would safeguard their bodies and minds during the long journey through the void. And they were promised that, upon reaching the ice-encrusted moon, they would awaken to a new world, ready to be shaped by their hands.

But the Terranauts were not the only precious cargo. Alongside them, nestled in the bowels of each launch facility, sat The Ark—a colossal vessel bearing not living creatures, but the very essence of Earth's biodiversity. Within its reinforced walls lay the DNA of every known animal and plant species, meticulously catalogued and preserved, ready to be cloned and brought to life once NovaTerra was deemed habitable. This genetic treasury was accompanied by the necessary equipment, containment facilities, and biological matter required to jumpstart a new ecosystem, one that would sustain and nourish the human settlers as they built their new home beneath the stars.

It was a staggering undertaking, a testament to human ingenuity and determination in the face of annihilation. But as the three-month countdown approached, a sense of trepidation hung heavy in the air. For all their meticulous planning and cutting-edge technology, the architects of NovaTerra knew that they were embarking on a journey into the unknown, a leap of faith that would determine the fate of their species. In the control room, all eyes were fixed on the screens, watching and waiting for the moment that would change everything.

CHAPTER 2
THE DREAMLESS VOYAGE

two

The Dreamless Voyage

Dr Vihaan Gupta sat in a small, sterile room, his heart racing with a mixture of anticipation and trepidation. The soft, white light emanating from the ceiling cast a gentle glow on his face, highlighting the flecks of grey in his dark hair and the lines of worry etched into his forehead. Across from him, Dr Amelia Chen, a young woman with a sharp intellect and a compassionate heart, studied a tablet intently, her brow furrowed in concentration. Her long, dark hair was pulled back into a neat ponytail, and her lab coat was crisp and white, a stark contrast to the dark circles under her eyes that hinted at countless late nights spent preparing for this moment.

"Dr Gupta," she began, looking up from the screen with a reassuring smile, "I'm Dr Amelia Chen, and I'll be guiding you through the pre-launch debriefing today."

Vihaan nodded, his mouth suddenly dry. "Thank you, Dr Chen. I have to admit, I'm feeling a little nervous about all of this."

Dr Chen's smile widened, her dark eyes filled with

understanding. "That's perfectly normal, Dr Gupta. What you're about to embark on is truly extraordinary, and it's only natural to have some apprehension. We're hoping that, after everything is explained, those of us taking our place in the pods will find our own reassurance in the three months prior to launch."

She tapped on the tablet, and a holographic display sprang to life between them, showing a detailed schematic of a sleek, silver pod. "This is the vessel that will carry you to Enceladus," she explained, her voice filled with pride. "We call it the TerraPod, and it represents the pinnacle of our engineering and technological capabilities."

Vihaan leaned forward, studying the intricate details of the pod. "It's incredible," he breathed, his eyes wide with wonder. "It's as I'd always imagined, yet somehow less science fiction and more credible."

Dr Chen nodded, her fingers dancing across the tablet's surface. "Indeed it is. But the true marvel lies in what will happen to you once you're inside."

The hologram shifted, revealing a human figure lying within the pod, surrounded by a shimmering, translucent field. "Prior to launch, the TerraPod will initiate the cryosleep process," Dr Chen continued, her voice taking on a more clinical tone. "This state of suspended animation will allow you to make the long journey to Enceladus without ageing or experiencing the passage of time."

Vihaan's brow furrowed, a flicker of concern crossing his face. "How can you be sure that I won't feel anything? That I won't be aware of the years slipping by?"

Dr Chen met his gaze, her expression one of deep conviction. "The cryosleep technology we've developed is the result of decades of research and testing. It works by dramatically slowing down your metabolic processes, essentially placing your body into a state of deep hibernation."

She tapped the tablet again, and the hologram zoomed in on the shimmering field surrounding the figure. "This is the key to the process," she explained, her voice filled with awe. "We call it 'vitrification,' and it involves the use of advanced cryoprotectants that prevent the formation of ice crystals within your cells. This ensures that your body remains perfectly preserved, without any damage or degradation."

Vihaan nodded slowly, trying to wrap his mind around the concept. "And my brain activity? Will I dream? Will I have any sense of the passage of time?"

Dr Chen shook her head, her expression one of gentle reassurance. "No, Dr Gupta. The cryosleep process will place your brain into a state of complete dormancy. You will have no dreams, no thoughts, no perception of the world around you. For all intents and purposes, you will be in a state of perfect, dreamless sleep."

She leaned forward, her eyes locking with Vihaan's. "I want you to understand, Dr Gupta, that we have taken every precaution to ensure your safety and well-being. The TerraPod is equipped with the most advanced life support systems ever created, constantly monitoring your vital signs and making adjustments as needed."

Vihaan took a deep breath, trying to calm his racing heart. "And when I arrive at Enceladus? How will I be awakened?"

Dr Chen smiled, a hint of excitement in her eyes. "The TerraPod is programmed to initiate the revival process automatically upon detecting the presence of a sustainable atmosphere. As you approach Enceladus, the pod will begin the gradual process of warming your body, slowly bringing your metabolic functions back to normal."

She paused, her expression growing more serious. "It's important to note that the revival process will take some time. Your body will need to adjust to the new environment, and you may experience some disorientation and weakness at first. But rest assured, our medical teams will be on hand to assist you every step of the way."

Vihaan nodded, a sense of determination settling over him. "I understand, Dr Chen. And I'm ready to do whatever it takes to ensure the success of the NovaTerra Project."

Dr Chen smiled, her eyes shining with admiration. "Your bravery and dedication are truly inspiring, Dr Gupta. You and your fellow Terranauts are the hope for our species, the ones who will carry the torch of humanity into a new era. I am proud, and honoured, to be part of this journey with you."

She stood, extending her hand to Vihaan. "On behalf of everyone at NovaTerra, I want to thank you for your sacrifice and your commitment. We will be with you every step of the way, monitoring your progress and ensuring that you arrive safely at your destination. I'm told that my launch will take place around fifteen minutes after yours."

Vihaan rose to his feet, grasping Dr Chen's hand firmly. "Thank you, Dr Chen. Your words mean more to me than you can imagine."

As he followed her out of the room, Vihaan's mind raced with thoughts of the journey ahead. He knew that the path he had chosen was one fraught with uncertainty and danger, but he also knew that it was the only hope for the survival of his species.

Stepping into the cavernous hangar bay, his eyes fell upon

the gleaming rows of TerraPods that would carry him and his fellow Terranauts to the stars. As they approached the sleek, silver vessels, Dr Chen began to explain more about their unique design.

"One of the most remarkable features of the TerraPod," she said, "is the observation deck. The top half of the pod is constructed from Aluminium Oxynitride, a transparent ceramic material that allows for 360-degree visibility. While this may seem unnecessary during cryosleep, it will serve as temporary housing once you reach Enceladus, providing shelter and a breathtaking view of your new home until permanent structures can be built."

Vihaan nodded, fascinated by the ingenuity of the design. "And what about power?" he asked. "How will we sustain ourselves on Enceladus?"

Dr Chen smiled. "The TerraPod is equipped with an electromagnetic drive system that allows for potentially infinite travel and serves as a detachable energy source. Upon awaking on Enceladus, you'll have immediate access to electricity, ensuring a smooth transition as you begin establishing the colony."

Vihaan felt a surge of pride and purpose. He was ready to face whatever lay ahead, to dream the dreamless sleep of the cryopod and awaken to a new world, a new beginning for all of humanity.

As they walked through the hangar bay, Vihaan suddenly stopped, a wave of guilt washing over him. He turned to Dr Chen, his eyes filled with a desperate plea. "Dr Chen, I know this may be an impossible request, but as one of the pioneers of the NovaTerra Project, is there any way that concessions could be made for me? My wife… she's everything to me, and

I can't bear the thought of leaving her behind to face the end alone."

Dr Chen's expression softened, a flicker of sympathy crossing her face. She placed a gentle hand on Vihaan's shoulder, her voice low and filled with understanding. "Dr Gupta, I know how difficult this must be for you. The bonds of love are the most powerful forces in the universe, and the thought of leaving your wife behind is an unimaginable sacrifice."

She took a deep breath, her eyes meeting Vihaan's with a solemn gaze. "But I'm afraid that the decision regarding the selection of Terranauts is above my pay grade. The process was incredibly meticulous, involving extensive research, background checks, and careful consideration of each individual's potential contribution to humanity's future on Enceladus."

Vihaan's shoulders slumped, a wave of despair washing over him. "Please, Dr Chen," he pleaded, his voice cracking with emotion. "There must be something you can do. I can't… I can't leave her behind."

Dr Chen's grip on his shoulder tightened, her own eyes glistening with unshed tears. "I wish I could help you, Dr Gupta. Truly, I do. But the harsh reality is that we have limited resources and space on the TerraPods. Every seat is precious, and every Terranaut was chosen for a specific reason."

She paused, her voice dropping to a whisper. "I know it's little consolation, but please know that your wife, like my husband, will be remembered as a hero. Her sacrifice, and yours, will be the foundation upon which a new future for humanity will be built."

Vihaan closed his eyes, a single tear rolling down his cheek. He took a shuddering breath, the weight of his decision settling heavily upon his shoulders. "I understand, Dr Chen," he said softly, his voice barely audible over the hum of machinery in the hangar bay. "I just... I needed to ask."

Dr Chen nodded, her own tears now flowing freely. "Of course, Dr Gupta. It's only natural to want to save those we love. But sometimes, the greatest act of love is letting go, knowing that their memory will live on through the work we do and the future we create."

Vihaan opened his eyes, a flicker of resolve burning through the grief and guilt. "You're right, Dr Chen. My wife... she would want me to be strong, to carry on the mission no matter the cost."

He straightened his shoulders, a newfound sense of purpose filling his heart. "I will carry her love with me to the stars, and I will make sure that her sacrifice was not in vain."

Dr Chen smiled through her tears, her admiration for Vihaan's strength and dedication evident in her gaze. "I have no doubt that you will, Dr Gupta. And we will be with you every step of the way, ensuring that her legacy, and yours, will endure for generations to come."

As they resumed their walk through the hangar bay, Vihaan's heart was heavy with the knowledge of all he would leave behind. The guilt and sorrow threatened to overwhelm him, but he clung to the tiny spark of hope that Dr Chen's words had ignited within him.

He knew that the path ahead would be fraught with challenges and uncertainties, and the thought of facing them without his beloved wife by his side was almost too much to bear. But he also knew that her love and sacrifice would be the driving force behind his every action, the guiding light that would lead him through the darkness of space and the unknown dangers of Enceladus.

As they approached the gleaming rows of TerraPods, Vihaan's mind raced with questions and doubts. What would life be like on the icy moon? Would the new colony succeed, or would they be doomed to failure and extinction, just like their counterparts on Earth? And how would he find the strength to carry on, knowing that he had left his wife behind to face the end alone?

Dr Chen's voice interrupted his thoughts, her tone filled with a mix of excitement and trepidation. "Dr Gupta, I know the road ahead is uncertain, and the sacrifices you're making are immense. But I want you to know that we have faith in you, and in the mission. We are the last hope for our species, the ones who will carry the torch of humanity into a new era."

Vihaan nodded, his jaw set with determination. He knew that the weight of the world rested on his shoulders, and the shoulders of his fellow Terranauts. But he also knew that he would not falter, would not let the sacrifices of his loved ones be in vain.

As they stood before the pods, the future of humanity waiting within their sleek, silver shells, Vihaan felt a surge of purpose and resolve. He would face the challenges ahead with courage and determination, armed with the love and memory of those he left behind.

For in the end, it was not just his own fate that hung in the balance, but the fate of his species, the fate of all he held dear. And he would not let them down, no matter the cost.

CHAPTER 3
SHIFTING HANDS

THREE

Shifting Hands

The control room was a hive of activity, a cacophony of voices and the incessant beeping of machinery filling the air. Dr Vihaan Gupta stood before a massive screen, his eyes scanning the data that flowed across its surface like a digital river. His heart raced as he read the latest reports, a sense of dread settling in the pit of his stomach.

"Dr Gupta!" a young technician called out, his voice tight with urgency. "We've just received an emergency alert from IASPEI. They're reporting unprecedented levels of volcanic unrest across the globe."

Vihaan's head snapped up, his gaze locking with the technician's. "What do you mean, unprecedented levels?"

The technician swallowed hard, his fingers flying across his keyboard as he pulled up a series of graphs and charts. "Seismic activity has increased tenfold in the past seventy-two hours. Gas emissions, thermal anomalies, ground deformation… it's all off the charts. They're saying it could be a precursor to a series of supervolcanic eruptions."

Vihaan's blood ran cold, his mind racing with the implications of such a catastrophic event. He turned back to the screen, his eyes scanning the data with renewed intensity. "Have we received any updates from NASA's Heliophysics Division?"

As if on cue, another alarm sounded, and a new data set began to flow across the screen. Vihaan's eyes widened as he read the report, his heart sinking with every word. "Dear God," he breathed, his voice barely above a whisper. "They're saying the volcanic activity could be triggered by a massive solar flare event. The energy output… it's unlike anything we've ever seen before."

The room fell silent, the weight of the news settling over the assembled scientists and technicians like a suffocating blanket. For a long moment, no one spoke; the only sound was the hum of the machines and the distant rumble of the ongoing launch preparations.

Finally, a voice broke the silence, calm and authoritative. It was Dr Lena Ivanov, her lips pressed into a thin line as she studied the data on the screen. "If these predictions are accurate," she said quietly, "we have no choice but to accelerate the launch timeline. We cannot afford to wait any longer."

Vihaan nodded, his mind already racing with the necessary calculations and adjustments. "How much time do we have?" he asked, his voice steady despite the fear that gripped his heart.

Dr Ivanov's gaze met his, her eyes filled with a grim determination. "Based on these readings, I'd say we have forty-eight hours at most before the first eruptions begin. Once the supervolcanoes start to erupt, the Earth will be consumed by fire and ash, making it impossible for us to launch the TerraPods. The debris and toxic gases in the atmosphere would make it too dangerous, and the seismic instability could damage the launch facilities beyond repair. If we don't get off the ground before then, we may never have another chance. After that..."

Vihaan turned to the room, his voice ringing out clear and strong. "You heard Dr Ivanov. We have forty-eight hours to get the TerraPods launched and our people off this planet. I want every department working around the clock to make the necessary preparations. We cannot afford a single mistake."

The room erupted into a frenzy of activity, technicians and scientists alike scrambling to their stations to begin the frantic work of readying the pods for launch. Vihaan stood at the centre of the maelstrom, his mind whirling with the enormity of the task before them.

He thought of his wife, of the billions of souls who would be left behind to face the coming apocalypse. The guilt and sorrow threatened to overwhelm him, but he pushed them aside, focusing instead on the mission at hand. He had a job to do, a sacred duty to ensure the survival of his species. And he would not fail them, not now, not ever.

As he turned back to the screen, his eyes scanning the data that continued to pour in from around the world, Vihaan felt a strange sense of calm settle over him. He knew that the road ahead would be fraught with danger and uncertainty and that the fate of humanity rested on the success of their mission. But he also knew that he was not alone, that he had the strength and courage of his fellow Terranauts beside him.

Together, they would face the gathering storm and ride the winds of fate to a new world, a new beginning. And though the journey would be long and the sacrifices great, Vihaan knew that it was the only path forward, the only hope for the future of his species.

He took a deep breath, his gaze fixed on the horizon as he

spoke, his voice a whisper against the chaos that swirled around him. "We will not fail. We cannot fail. For the sake of all we hold dear, we will find a way."

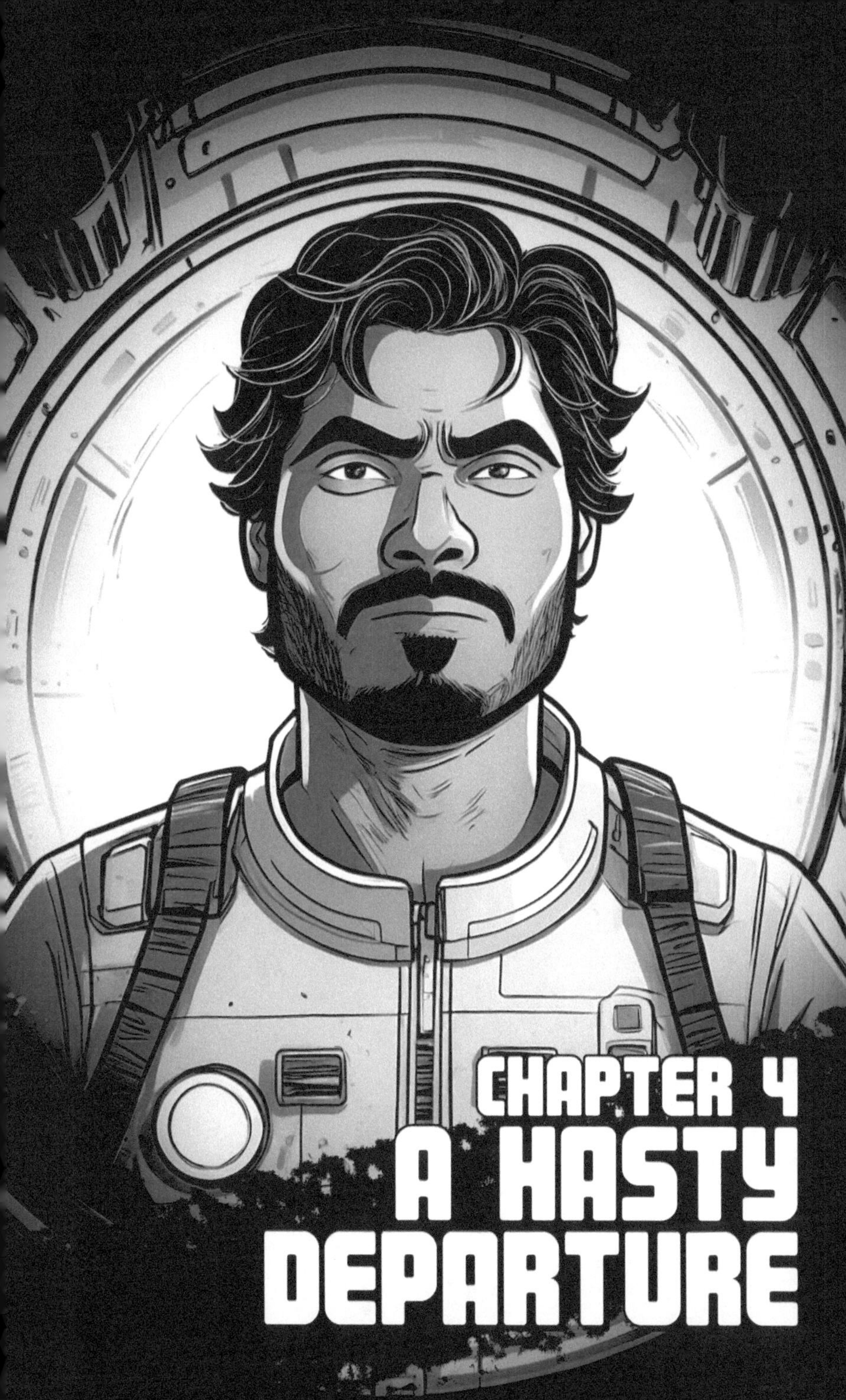
CHAPTER 4
A HASTY
DEPARTURE

FOUR

A Hasty Departure

The hangar bay buzzed with a frenetic energy, the air crackling with tension and anticipation. The launch day, once a distant milestone on the NovaTerra Project's carefully crafted timeline, had been abruptly moved forward by three months due to the looming threat of solar flares and the alarming increase in supervolcanic activity. The sudden acceleration of the schedule had sent shockwaves through the ranks of the scientists and engineers, forcing them to work around the clock to prepare the TerraPods and their precious cargo for the journey ahead.

Vihaan could feel the weight of the moment pressing down on him as he strode towards his designated pod, his heart pounding in his chest. He knew that the hasty departure was a necessary evil, a last-ditch effort to ensure the survival of the human species in the face of an impending cataclysm. But he couldn't shake the nagging feeling that they were cutting it too close, that the mad scramble to launch the pods had left too many variables unaccounted for.

As he approached the gleaming silver vessel that would carry him across the vast reaches of space, Vihaan took a moment to marvel at its sleek, futuristic design. The TerraPod was a testament to the ingenuity and determination of the NovaTerra Project's team, a marvel of engineering that pushed the boundaries of what was thought possible.

The pod's exterior was constructed from a revolutionary material known as Carbenium, a hybrid of carbon fibre and Rhenium that had been painstakingly engineered to withstand the extreme conditions of space travel. The unique combination of materials, coupled with the cutting-edge chemical vapour deposition technique used to craft the shell, allowed the TerraPod to maintain its structural integrity even at temperatures reaching 6000 degrees Fahrenheit.

But it was the pod's interior that truly showcased the depth of thought and planning that had gone into its design. As Vihaan climbed inside, he was greeted by a dizzying array of advanced technology, from the banks of computers and monitoring equipment lining the walls to the sophisticated life support systems that would keep him alive and protected throughout the long journey.

At the heart of the pod lay the cryochamber, a gleaming white capsule that would serve as Vihaan's sanctuary for the next eight years. The chamber was a marvel of bioengineering, equipped with an array of sensors and regulators that would maintain the delicate balance of the cryosleep process, keeping his body in a state of suspended animation until the pod reached its distant destination.

As he settled into the cryochamber, Vihaan's thoughts drifted to the other vital component of the NovaTerra Project: The Ark. This massive, self-contained biosphere represented a bold attempt to preserve the rich tapestry of Earth's biodiversity, a living library of the countless species that had evolved and thrived on the planet's surface over millions of years.

Vihaan couldn't help but feel a sense of awe and gratitude towards the project's visionary leaders, who had recognised the importance of safeguarding not just human life but the entire web of existence that had sustained and enriched it for so long. He shuddered to think of how easy it would have been to overlook the critical role that Earth's creatures played in maintaining the delicate balance of its ecosystems, to focus solely on the survival of the human species at the expense of all else.

As the hatch of the TerraPod sealed shut with a soft hiss, Vihaan took a moment to gaze through the transparent Aluminium Oxynitride canopy, marvelling at the bustling activity in the hangar bay. He watched as his fellow Terranauts took their places in their own pods, their faces a mix of excitement, fear, and determination.

Vihaan felt a renewed sense of purpose and determination wash over him. He knew that the road ahead would be fraught with challenges and uncertainties, that the hastily accelerated launch schedule had left them little room for error or second-guessing.

But he also knew that he was part of something greater than himself, a project that carried the hopes and dreams of an entire planet on its shoulders. And as he sat in the stillness of his pod, he silently vowed to do everything in his power to ensure the success of the mission, to honor the sacrifices and the vision of all those who had made it possible.

For in the end, the TerraPod was more than just a vessel of hope, more than just a cradle of humanity. It was a symbol of the indomitable spirit of a species that refused to surrender to the darkness, that dared to reach for the stars even as its world crumbled beneath its feet. And with that knowledge burning bright in his heart, Vihaan prepared himself for the launch, ready to embark on the most important journey of his life.

CHAPTER 5
A DREAM INTERRUPTED

FIVE

A Dream Interrupted

"T-minus ten seconds."

The metallic voice of the automated launch sequence filled the cramped confines of Vihaan's TerraPod, each word a thunderous reminder of the momentous journey that lay ahead. Vihaan's heart raced with a potent mixture of excitement and trepidation, his mind struggling to grasp the enormity of the task before him.

"Nine."

As the countdown continued, Vihaan's thoughts drifted to the countless hours of preparation and training that had led him to this moment. The rigorous physical and psychological evaluations, the endless simulations and drills, the sacrifices and compromises that had shaped his life for as long as he could remember.

"Eight."

A sudden flare of light caught Vihaan's eye, and he turned his gaze upward, his breath catching in his throat at the sight that greeted him. The sky above the launch facility was alight with a dazzling display of solar flares, their tendrils of energy reaching out across the heavens like the fingers of some cosmic deity.

"Seven."

The sight was at once mesmerising and terrifying, a powerful reminder of the raw, untamed forces that governed the universe. Vihaan felt a shiver run down his spine as he contemplated the sheer magnitude of the journey that lay ahead, the countless light-years that separated him from his ultimate destination.

"Six."

As the intensity of the solar flares increased, Vihaan's excitement began to give way to a creeping sense of unease. He knew that the TerraPod had been designed to withstand the rigours of space travel, that its advanced shielding and life support systems would protect him from the worst of the cosmic radiation and gravitational stresses.

"Five."

But as the countdown neared its end and the moment of

launch drew ever closer, Vihaan couldn't shake the feeling that something was amiss. The solar flares were growing stronger by the second, their light so intense that it was almost blinding even through the heavily tinted viewing port of his pod.

"Four."

Suddenly, Vihaan felt a cold sensation wash over his body, a numbing chill that seemed to emanate from the very depths of his being. He recognised it instantly as the onset of cryosleep, the artificial hibernation process that would preserve his body and mind during the long journey through the void.

As the cryosleep took hold and his thoughts began to drift into a hazy, dreamlike state, Vihaan struggled to hold onto the last vestiges of his waking consciousness. He had so many questions, so many doubts and fears that he longed to voice aloud. But the words wouldn't come, his tongue leaden and unresponsive as the icy grip of cryosleep tightened around his mind.

"Three."

The world outside Vihaan's pod had faded to a distant, muffled drone, the countdown and the roar of the launch engines blending together into a single, indistinguishable hum. He felt as though he were floating in a vast, empty void, his body weightless and insubstantial as he drifted deeper into the embrace of cryosleep.

"Two."

In the final moments before the launch, Vihaan's mind conjured up a fleeting image of his loved ones back on Earth. His wife, his mother, his siblings—all the people he had left behind in pursuit of this grand, audacious dream. He wanted to reach out to them, to tell them one last time how much he loved them, how grateful he was for their support and sacrifice.

"One."

But it was too late. As the final number of the countdown echoed through the confines of his pod, Vihaan felt the last remnants of his consciousness slip away, his thoughts fragmenting and dissolving like mist in the morning sun. He was dimly aware of a sudden surge of acceleration, a powerful force that seemed to press him back against the cushioned surface of his cryochamber.

And then, silence. Darkness. A vast, yawning emptiness that seemed to stretch out into eternity.

***

Unbeknownst to Vihaan, lost in the depths of cryosleep, a drama of unimaginable proportions was unfolding outside the confines of his pod. One by one, the other TerraPods rose from their launch supports, their sleek, silver forms glistening in the otherworldly light of the solar flares that danced across the sky.

From the remote control centre, they watched with bated breath as the first pod, carrying the leader of the free world, lifted off from the Utah facility and hurtled towards the heavens. Moments later, the rest of the pods followed suit, their launches synchronised with precision and grace, even as the Sun's fury threatened to engulf them all.

The solar flares, born in the heart of the Sun at temperatures reaching millions of degrees Fahrenheit, raced across the void, their energy undiminished by the vast expanse of space. By the time they reached Earth, these tendrils of destruction still carried the heat of tens of thousands of degrees, their power equal to that of millions of nuclear explosions. As they collided with the planet's upper atmosphere, they set the very air ablaze, turning the sky into a cauldron of fire and plasma.

As the pods reached the edge of Earth's atmosphere, disaster struck. A monstrous solar flare, larger and more intense than any that had come before, erupted from the surface of the Sun, its searing fingers reaching out to embrace the fleeing vessels like the arms of some vengeful god.

One by one, the pods were consumed by the relentless heat and radiation of the solar flare, their fragile forms crumbling like paper in a furnace. The president's pod was the first to succumb, followed in quick succession by the rest of the fleet, until only a single vessel remained, a lonely survivor in the face of annihilation.

Vihaan's pod, by some miracle of chance or design, had been thrown off course by the impact of the solar flare, its trajectory altered just enough to carry it clear of the worst of the maelstrom. But even as it sped away into the darkness of space, its occupant remained blissfully unaware of the chaos and destruction that had unfolded around him.

For Vihaan, lost in the dreamless slumber of cryosleep, the journey had only just begun—a journey that would take him far beyond the reach of Earth and its dying civilisations into the vast, uncharted reaches of the cosmos, where the fate of humanity and the secrets of the universe awaited him with open arms as he slept.

CHAPTER 6
THE ETERNAL
OBSERVER

SIX

The Eternal Observer

Vihaan's eyes snapped open, his mind suddenly wrenched from the void of cryosleep by a force he couldn't comprehend. It took him a moment to realise that the violent jolt that had awoken him was the result of a massive solar flare, its energy so intense that it had penetrated the pod's shielding and disrupted the delicate balance of the vitrification process.

He tried to move, to cry out in confusion and terror, but his body remained utterly paralysed, a frozen prison of flesh and bone. The vitrification had completely halted his metabolism, locking him in a state of unchanging stasis. However, it had done nothing to stop the relentless workings of his mind.

Panic and despair surged through Vihaan's thoughts as he struggled to make sense of his situation. He wanted to scream, to pound on the walls of his pod until someone, anyone, heard him and came to his aid. But his cries were trapped inside his own head, his pleas for help nothing more than silent echoes in the void.

Suddenly, the pod's onboard computer burst into life, its

calm, automated voice a jarring contrast to the chaos of Vihaan's thoughts. "*All systems normal*," it reported, oblivious to the waking nightmare unfolding within the cryochamber. "*Current trajectory: altered. Estimated time to destination: unknown.*"

Altered trajectory? Unknown destination? The words sent a fresh wave of fear coursing through Vihaan's mind. What had happened to the other pods, to the rest of the NovaTerra mission? Had they suffered the same fate as him, their occupants condemned to an eternity of waking paralysis?

As if in answer to his unspoken questions, the pod's viewscreens flickered to life, painting a terrifying tableau across the curved expanse of the cryochamber. Vihaan's eyes widened in horror as he beheld the fate of his homeworld, the only reality he had ever known.

Earth hung in the void like a wounded animal, its surface ravaged by the scars of a thousand volcanic eruptions. The once-blue planet was now a mottled patchwork of grey and black, its oceans boiled away, and its continents reduced to ash and ruin.

And in the distance, the remains of the other TerraPods drifted like shattered toys, their hulls twisted and blackened by the fury of the solar flare. Vihaan's mind reeled at the sight, his thoughts spinning with the realisation that he was now truly alone, a solitary survivor adrift in the endless expanse of space.

But even that horrifying revelation paled in comparison to what came next. As Vihaan watched, transfixed by the apocalyptic scene unfolding before him, a second flare erupted from the surface of the Sun, a gargantuan tongue of plasma that seemed to dwarf even the mightiest of prior eruptions.

The flare arced across the void with impossible speed, its

tendrils of energy enveloping the Earth and its moon in a deadly embrace. For a moment, the two celestial bodies seemed to glow from within, their surfaces transformed into incandescent seas of fire and light.

And then, with a soundless flash that seared itself into Vihaan's retinas, they simply vanished, consumed by the all-devouring hunger of the Sun. Vihaan's mind went blank with shock and disbelief, his thoughts fragmenting into a thousand shards of jagged, uncomprehending hysteria.

He was alone now, truly and utterly alone, a forgotten relic of a species that had been wiped from the cosmos in the blink of an eye. The realisation settled over him like a leaden shroud—a suffocating weight that pressed down on his paralysed form with merciless intensity.

Time lost all meaning as Vihaan drifted through the void, his pod carrying him ever further from the shattered remains of his homeworld. His thoughts spun in endless, recursive loops, his mind grappling with the enormity of his loss and the terrifying uncertainty of his future.

Where would he end up, he wondered, his silent cries echoing in the chambers of his skull. Would he find some new world to call home, some distant oasis of life and warmth amidst the cold and empty wastes of space? Or would he drift forever, a frozen ghost condemned to an eternity of waking death?

The onboard computer burst into life once more, its voice an incongruous intrusion into Vihaan's spiralling thoughts. "*All systems normal,*" it reported, as if anything about his situation could be considered normal. But the next words sent a fresh jolt of shock through Vihaan's paralysed body.

"*Current date: 2241.*"

Two hundred years? He had been adrift for almost two centuries, his body frozen in an unchanging prison of flesh and bone while the universe moved on without him. The realisation was like a physical blow, a knife twisting in his gut with cruel, relentless precision.

Despair and madness loomed at the edges of Vihaan's consciousness, their icy fingers reaching out to ensnare his fragile grasp on sanity. But even as he teetered on the brink of oblivion, some small, stubborn part of him refused to surrender, refused to accept the hopelessness of his fate.

And so he raged against the dying of the light, his silent screams echoing through the empty chambers of his mind as he clung to the fading embers of his humanity. He would endure, he vowed, even if it meant an eternity of frozen isolation and unending torment. He would bear witness to the passing of the ages, a solitary sentinel watching over the ruins of a shattered universe.

For in the end, that was all he had left: the grim, unyielding determination to survive, to carry the memory of Earth and its lost children into the unknown reaches of the cosmos. And with that thought burning like a cold fire in the depths of his being, Vihaan surrendered himself once more to the endless dance of the stars, a frozen scream echoing silently in the vast, uncaring void. Waiting. Hoping.

CHAPTER 7
A DREAM OF DEATH

SEVEN

A Dream of Death

As the centuries turned to millennia and the millennia to aeons, Vihaan's mind wandered the labyrinthine paths of his consciousness, his thoughts the only companions in his endless journey through the void. The once-sharp edges of his sanity had long since worn away, eroded by the relentless passage of time and the crushing weight of his isolation.

He pondered the nature of his predicament, his mind grasping at fleeting straws of half-remembered knowledge and long-forgotten theories. He recalled a strange quirk of human perception, a curious tendency of the mind to deceive itself when deprived of external cues and references.

If a blindfolded person tried to walk in a straight line, they would inevitably drift off course, their path curving back on itself in a vain attempt to maintain a sense of direction. In many cases, they would end up returning to their starting point, their minds convinced that they had travelled a great distance in a single, unbroken line.

Could the same principle apply to his pod? Might its trajectory bend and warp imperceptibly, causing it to return to the point of origin—the scorched remains of Earth?

But what would be the point, he mused bleakly. Earth was gone, consumed by the fury of the Sun, its once-teeming surface now nothing more than a scorched and lifeless husk.

And even if he could somehow alter course toward Enceladus, what hope did he have of surviving the journey? His body was a frozen prison, his mind a shattered relic of a now-vanished species, a living fossil adrift in the cosmos—a forgotten remnant of a world that had long since passed into memory and myth.

Suddenly, the onboard computer crackled to life once more, its voice an eerie echo of a time long past. "*All systems normal,*" it reported, its tone as maddeningly calm as ever. But the next words sent a jolt of unadulterated terror through Vihaan's ancient, atrophied frame.

"*Current date: 4,022,037 AD*"

Millions of years. He had been adrift in the void for aeons, his consciousness a flickering spark against the vast, unending darkness of space. The realisation hit like a physical blow, a wave of vertigo and disbelief threatening to overwhelm his fragile grasp on reality.

But then, even as despair and madness clawed at the edges of his mind, Vihaan felt an impossible sensation ripple through his frozen muscles. His mouth, long paralysed by the unending grip of vitrification, twitched in the faintest approximation of a sigh—the first voluntary movement in countless millennia.

Excitement surged through his mind, a wild, desperate hope long abandoned. With titanic effort, he focused on his jaw, teeth, and tongue, willing them to obey his commands. He attempted to move his tongue, to form words, but found only a hollow void where it had once been, the muscle having long since wasted away or inexplicably dissolved in the interminable ages of his confinement.

Slowly, painfully, he began to click his teeth together in a halting, staccato rhythm, his mind dredging up long-forgotten memories of Morse code. Each click sent a fresh wave of agony lancing through atrophied muscles, but he pressed on, driven by a desperate, all-consuming need to make contact, to reach out across the vast, empty gulf of space and time.

"Send help," he tapped out, his jaw aching with each precise, deliberate movement. "All alone. I am the last one to live."

A pensive pause stretched out into an eternity of waiting and hoping. And then, a final, wrenching effort as Vihaan spelt out the bleak truth of his existence, an epitaph echoing across the cosmos like a dying star's final lament:

"I dream of death."

With those words, Vihaan felt the last embers of his consciousness begin to gutter and dim, his mind slipping into the welcoming embrace of oblivion. He had borne witness to the passing of ages and watched the birth and death of countless stars.

But in the end, even his stubborn, unyielding will to endure had reached its limit, eroded by the unimaginable weight of aeons. As awareness faded, Vihaan felt a final, fleeting moment of clarity amidst the chaos and madness of his existence.

Perhaps this was his true purpose, he mused, his thoughts growing dim and distant as the darkness closed in. Not to carry the seed of humanity to some distant world, but to serve as a living testament to the indomitable spirit of his species, to the unquenchable fire that had driven them to reach for the stars even in the face of annihilation.

And with that comforting thought, Vihaan surrendered himself to the infinite void, his consciousness dissolving into the vast, eternal symphony of the universe. He had dreamed of life, had fought and endured beyond all reason and hope.

Now, the dream of death welcomed him home at last—a final, merciful release from the bonds of his frozen, unchanging prison. His story would live on, whispered in the echoes of his repeating, fading signal, a quantum memorial to the sheer, stubborn will to survive that had carried his species from the savannas of Africa to the very edge of an unknown universe.

And so Vihaan, the last Terranaut, drifted forever through the currents of space and time—a silent observer in the vast, unending cycle of creation and destruction. Alone, but never truly alone. A dreamer of death, embraced by eternity.

L to R: Micah Snow (guitars), Baz Fitzsimmons (guitars), Mark Reid (vocals), Chris Horne (bass), Mark Riches (drums)

TANTRUM, a Glasgow-based old-school metal band, has been captivating audiences with their classic guitar-driven riffs and driving rhythms since 2014. The band's evolution has been marked by significant turning points, including the introduction of stronger lyrical themes, thought-provoking content, and solid vocal harmonies to their music in 2021.

TANTRUM's sound has grown heavier and more modern while retaining the accessibility that fans have come to love. The band's current powerhouse ensemble has reinforced their newfound lyrical depth and musical prowess, delivering intense and dynamic performances that showcase their growth.

With their bold, innovative approach and commanding stage presence, TANTRUM has established themselves as a force to be reckoned with in the metal scene.

TANTRUM
"No Place for the Damned" CD
Buy now from tantrum.rocks using the QR code shown to the right >
TANTRUM
NO PLACE FOR THE DAMNED
TANTRUM
NO PLACE FOR THE DAMNED
TRINITY EDITION
TANTRUM
"No Place for the Damned"
Trinity Edition CD
Buy now from tantrum.rocks using the QR code shown to the left <

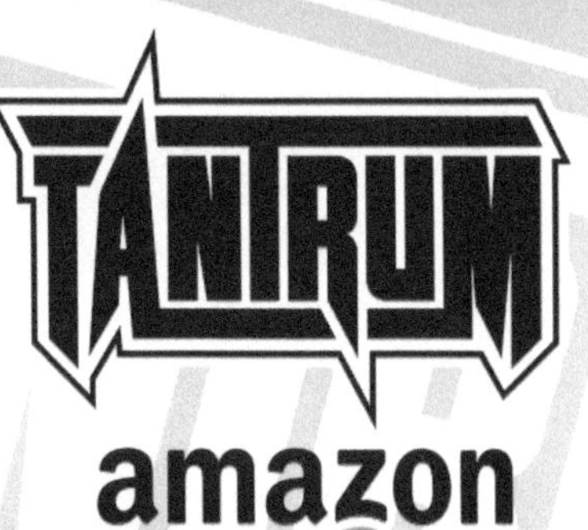

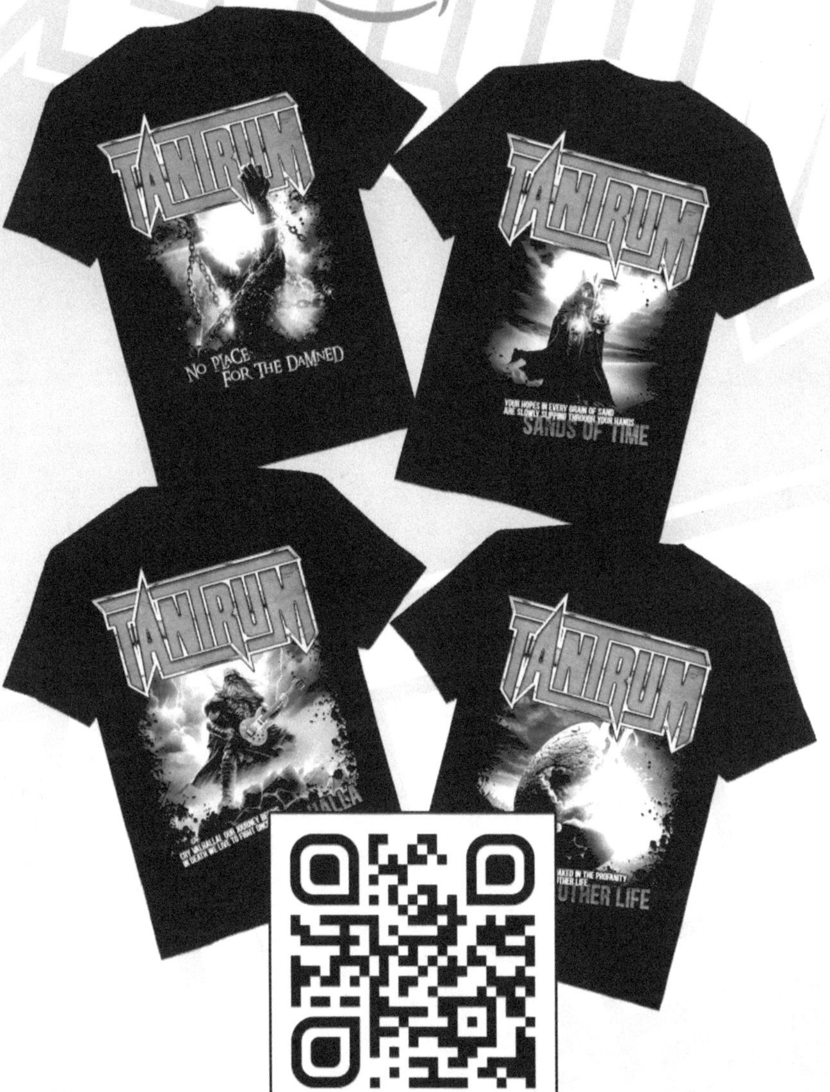
TANTRUM
NO PLACE
FOR THE DAMNED
TANTRUM
YOUR HOPES IN EVERY GRAIN OF SAND
ARE SLOWLY SLIPPING THROUGH YOUR HANDS
SANDS OF TIME
TANTRUM
TANTRUM

www.ingramcontent.com/pod-product-compliance
Lightning Source LLC
LaVergne TN
LVHW040944150826
845672LV00002B/524

* 9 7 8 1 9 1 2 3 2 5 3 4 4 *